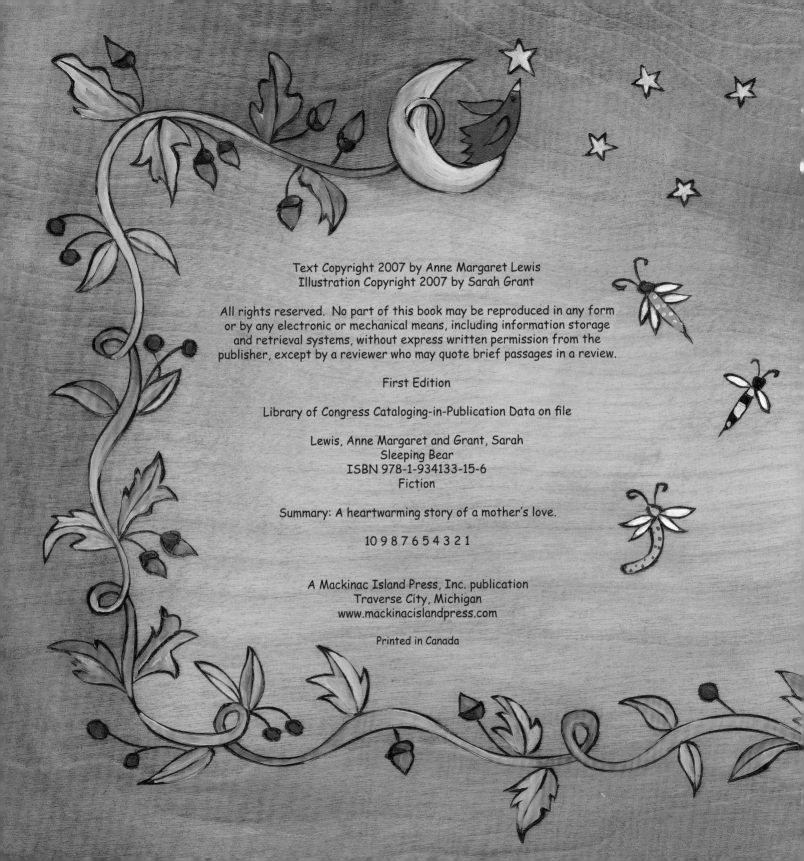

First Edition

Library of Congress Cataloging-in-Publication Data on file

Lewis, Anne Margaret and Grant, Sarah
Sleeping Bear
ISBN 978-1-934133-15-6
Fiction

Summary: A heartwarming story of a mother's love.

10 9 8 7 6 5 4 3 2 1

A Mackinac Island Press, Inc. publication
Traverse City, Michigan
www.mackinacislandpress.com

Printed in Canada

Sleeping Bear
The Legend

by Anne Margaret Lewis
art by Sarah Grant

Many, many
moons ago
in a land of the
great tall trees,

lived
two little cubs
and their Momma Bear,
who would frolic
among
the
leaves.

They lived
in a land
called Wishkons

in a woods near
the big, big lake.

These woods were filled
with animals—
with deer and
skunks and snakes.

The cubs
danced and played
with friends
all day,

chasing fox and
bunnies and squirrels.

At the close of each day
they returned to their den,
back to Momma Bear
and their safe little world.

Honey

They snoozed
and snored
with no care in the world,
sleeping soundly beneath
star-filled skies.
When dawn appeared
with the sweet morning dew,
Mr. Sun
sang a song
"Time to Rise...

...chase butterflies

...hear chattering magpies

...eat picnic surprise."

One beautiful
sunny day,
when the sky
was as clear
as a bell,
the cubs
wandered off
in their chase,

until they heard Momma Bear
sternly yell!

"No time for playful games,"
she said
with her eyebrows
tightly furrowed.

"You must stay right
near my side."
"we will,"
the cubs softly
echoed.

The animals
stayed together –
squirrels,
fox,
and even Possum the Pest.
Some weren't as fast
as the others,

but they all waited...never-the-less.

Mr. Turtle
brought
up the rear.
They spotted
Lake Michigama's
shore.

They hurried into the
cold, cold lake –
Momma Bear
and her two baby cubs,
heading toward a land called
Michigama
with their
never-ending love.

As
Momma Bear
reached
the shore,

she gazed over the
blanket of blue –
"Guide and guard my cubs!"
she pleaded,
to the Great Spirit Manitou.

She lay there with
hope and devotion
through winter,
spring,
summer
and
fall.

" Thank you, Great Spirit !"
Momma Bear cried.
"You watched over my baby cubs."

This book is dedicated to...

with love from

Anne Margaret Lewis

Award winning author Anne Margaret Lewis has been writing children's books since the sixth grade when she 'wrote, designed, and published' her first children's book. It is her natural imagination that has inspired her to continue on to work with lighthouses, fireflies, bears, a very cute elf named Emit, and the great Gitchi Gumee. Her stories have charming characters, inspirational themes, and subtle, yet important messages.

Anne Margaret, is the mother of four wonderful children, Caitlin, Matthew, Patrick and Cameron, and loves to share her passion for writing and reading with children in schools throughout the country. Born and raised in Michigan, Anne Margaret Lewis is a graduate of the University of Michigan, and lives on a magical peninsula in Northern Michigan with her husband, Brian, and children, where she continues to write and imagine.

Sarah Grant

Born in Rochester, New York, in 1953, is the talented and charismatic artist and mother Sarah Grant. She was raised in Ames, Iowa, and is the oldest of three siblings. Sarah presently resides in Des Moines, Iowa, and is the mother of three beautiful daughters, Rachel, Rebecca and Hannah. Sarah is an abstract painter and the founder and owner of Sticks, Inc., a nationally recognized creator of artistic furniture, accessories and object art. It is her adoration and devotion to a life filled with education, learning and creativity that has gained her national recognition. Sarah holds a Bachelor of Fine Arts in Drawing and Printmaking, a Masters in Printmaking, and a Masters of Fine Arts in Painting from the University of Iowa. Sarah Grant's paintings and Sticks creations are represented in museum, corporate, private and public collections as well as galleries across the country.